J
2nd
YILLENEUVE

1495

A Note to Parents and Caregivers:

Read-it! Readers are for children who are just starting on the amazing road to reading. These beautiful books support both the acquisition of reading skills and the love of books.

 The PURPLE LEVEL presents basic topics and objects using high frequency words and simple language patterns.

 The RED LEVEL presents familiar topics using common words and repeating sentence patterns.

 The BLUE LEVEL presents new ideas using a larger vocabulary and varied sentence structure.

 The YELLOW LEVEL presents more challenging ideas, a broad vocabulary, and wide variety in sentence structure.

 The GREEN LEVEL presents more complex ideas, an extended vocabulary range, and expanded language structures.

 The ORANGE LEVEL presents a wide range of ideas and concepts using challenging vocabulary and complex language structures.

When sharing a book with your child, read in short stretches, pausing often to talk about the pictures. Have your child turn the pages and point to the pictures and familiar words. And be sure to reread favorite stories or parts of stories.

There is no right or wrong way to share books with children. Find time to read with your child, and pass on the legacy of literacy.

Adria F. Klein, Ph.D.
Professor Emeritus
California State University
San Bernardino, California

To Uncle Bert

First American edition published in 2005 by
Picture Window Books
5115 Excelsior Boulevard
Suite 232
Minneapolis, MN 55416
877-845-8392
www.picturewindowbooks.com

First published in Canada in 2001 by
Les éditions Héritage inc.
300 Arran Street, Saint Lambert
Quebec, Canada J4R 1K5

Printed in the United States of America.

Library of Congress Cataloging-in-Publication Data
Villeneuve, Mireille.
Mysteries for Felicio / Mireille Villeneuve ; [illustrated by] Anne Villeneuve.
p. cm. — (Read-it! readers)
Summary: Felicio's father does not believe in the tooth fairy, the sandman, or Santa Claus, but after a few mishaps such as losing a molar, and with his son's help, he quickly changes his mind.
ISBN 1-4048-1033-1 (hardcover)
[1. Fathers and sons—Fiction. 2. Tooth Fairy—Fiction. 3. Sandman—Fiction.
4. Santa Claus—Fiction.] I. Villeneuve, Anne, ill. II. Title. III. Series.

PZ7.V73My 2004
[E]—dc22   2004023777

Mysteries for Felicio

By Mireille Villeneuve
Illustrated by Anne Villeneuve

Special thanks to our advisers for their expertise:

Adria F. Klein, Ph.D.
Professor Emeritus, California State University
San Bernardino, California

Susan Kesselring, M.A.
Literacy Educator
Rosemount - Apple Valley - Eagan (Minnesota) School District

PICTURE WINDOW BOOKS
Minneapolis, Minnesota

Felicio's father was really very funny. He had 12 clown costumes and a drawer full of fake noses. One morning, Mr. Bartholemy dressed as Rigoletto the Clown to go to work.

Then he went into the
kitchen and helped himself
to a big bowl of cereal.
He took enormous
mouthfuls and made a lot
of noise: Crunch! Crunch!
CRRUNK!?!

Oh no! He had just
chomped on the surprise in
the cereal box! Clink!
A shiny white molar fell
on the floor.

"Yow! I've lost a tooth!"
howled Mr. Bartholemy.

Felicio told his father not to worry.
Felicio promised that the tooth fairy
would come and visit Mr. Bartholemy.
She would take his old tooth and leave
a nice new penny in its place.

"Come on, Felicio! There's no such thing as the tooth fairy," said his father, laughing hard.

Felicio's grandmother had been listening. She shook a finger under Mr. Bartholemy's nose and said, "The tooth fairy only visits people who believe in her. Too bad for you!"

That night, Felicio put on a funny disguise. He tiptoed into his father's bedroom. Then, lifting a corner of the pillow, he placed a shiny new penny on the sheet.

But that was odd—it seemed as if someone else had already done the same thing!

The next morning, Mr. Bartholemy
found two shiny pennies under
his pillow. He was very surprised.
And so was Felicio!

From then on, Mr. Bartholemy
believed in the tooth fairy.

But Felicio's father had another problem. In the morning, his eyes were always red and tired-looking. It had to be because his father went to bed too late, thought Felicio. He warned his father:

"If you don't go to bed on time, the sandman will visit you!"

"The sandman! Ha! Ha!"
snickered Mr. Bartholemy.

Felicio drew a picture of the terrible fellow on his blackboard. But it did no good. His father refused to believe in the sandman. However, Felicio knew the sandman really did exist.

Later that night, Mr. Bartholemy
was visited by a scary creature.
Quick! Quick! He ran and hid under
his blankets. And so did Felicio!

From then on, Mr. Bartholemy and
Felicio went to bed early.

The next day was the Santa Claus
parade. Felicio asked his father to
come with him.

But Mr. Bartholemy didn't believe in
Santa Claus. Felicio's grandmother had
to drag his father along with them.

It was Mr. Bartholemy's turn to sit on Santa's lap. The jolly old man asked him what he wanted for Christmas. Everyone strained their ears.

But Mr. Bartholemy was so shy that he whispered in a tiny voice:

"I'd like ..."

No one had heard—
except, of course, Santa Claus!

On Christmas morning, Felicio
was awakened by a funny kind of
Santa Claus.

He had a present for everyone in his sack.

Suddenly, there was a loud
BOOM! Another present had
just come down the chimney.

A little card attached to the
present said:

> To Mr. Bartholemy,
> From Santa Claus.

Felicio's father opened the mysterious package. "Oh! Fantastic!" he said. "It's a squirt gun— just what I asked Santa for!" He couldn't believe his eyes. Neither could Felicio's grandmother!

"I have a present for you, too,"
Felicio told his father.

It was an enormous storybook,
full of fairies, sandmen, elves,
and Santas.

Mr. Bartholemy was delighted.
And so was Felicio!

31

More *Read-it!* Readers

Bright pictures and fun stories help you practice your reading skills. Look for more books at your level.

Alex and the Team Jersey by Gilles Tibo
Alex and Toolie by Gilles Tibo
Clever Cat by Karen Wallace
Daddy's a Busy Beaver by Bruno St-Aubin
Daddy's a Dinosaur by Bruno St-Aubin
Felicio's Incredible Invention by Mireille Villeneuve
Flora McQuack by Penny Dolan
Izzie's Idea by Jillian Powell
Mysteries for Felicio by Mireille Villeneuve
Naughty Nancy by Anne Cassidy
Parents Do the Weirdest Things! by Louise Tondreau-Levert
Peppy, Patch, and the Postman by Marisol Sarrazin
Peppy, Patch, and the Socks by Marisol Sarrazin
The Princess and the Frog by Margaret Nash
The Roly-Poly Rice Ball by Penny Dolan
Run! by Sue Ferraby
Sausages! by Anne Adeney
Stickers, Shells, and Snow Globes by Dana Meachen Rau
Theodore the Millipede by Carole Tremblay
The Truth About Hansel and Gretel by Karina Law
Willie the Whale by Joy Oades

Looking for a specific title or level? A complete list of *Read-it!* Readers is available on our Web site: *www.picturewindowbooks.com*